Topsy-Turvy Town

By Luc Melanson

J
Picture Bk
Melanson

TUNDRA BOOKS

Published in Canada by Tundra Books,
75 Sherbourne Street, Toronto, Ontario M5A 2P9

Published in the United States by Tundra Books of Northern New York,
P.O. Box 1030, Plattsburgh, New York 12901

Library of Congress Control Number: 2009929059

LIBRARY AND ARCHIVES CANADA CATALOGUING IN PUBLICATION

Melanson, Luc
[Ma drôle de ville. English]
    Topsy-turvy town / Luc Melanson.

Translation of: Ma drôle de ville.
ISBN 978-0-88776-920-7

    I. Title. II. Title: Ma drôle de ville. English.

PS8626.E42M3213 2010   jC843'.6   C2009-903216-3

We acknowledge the financial support of the Government of Canada through the Book Publishing Industry Development Program and that of the Government of Ontario through the Ontario Media Development Corporation's Ontario Book Initiative. We further acknowledge the support of the Canada Council for the Arts and the Ontario Arts Council for our publishing program.

ONTARIO ARTS COUNCIL
CONSEIL DES ARTS DE L'ONTARIO

Printed in China

1 2 3 4 5 6   15 14 13 12 11 10

For Marie-Claude and our two children's tremendous imaginations

– L.M.

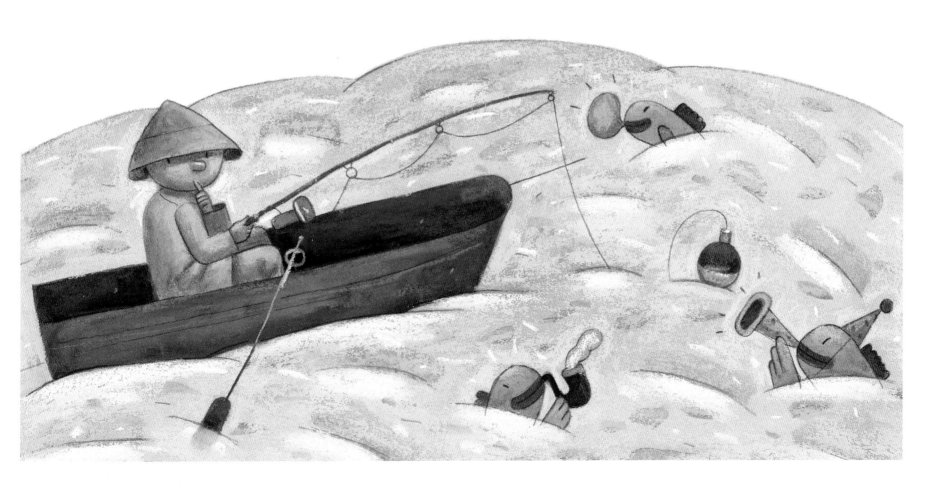

I live in Topsy-Turvy Town.

My sister says that's silly,

but it's my favorite place to be.

In Topsy-Turvy Town, it rains broccoli that bounces off umbrellas and makes an awful crunch.

The cars are made of chocolate with pineapple wheels.
They are yummy to eat.

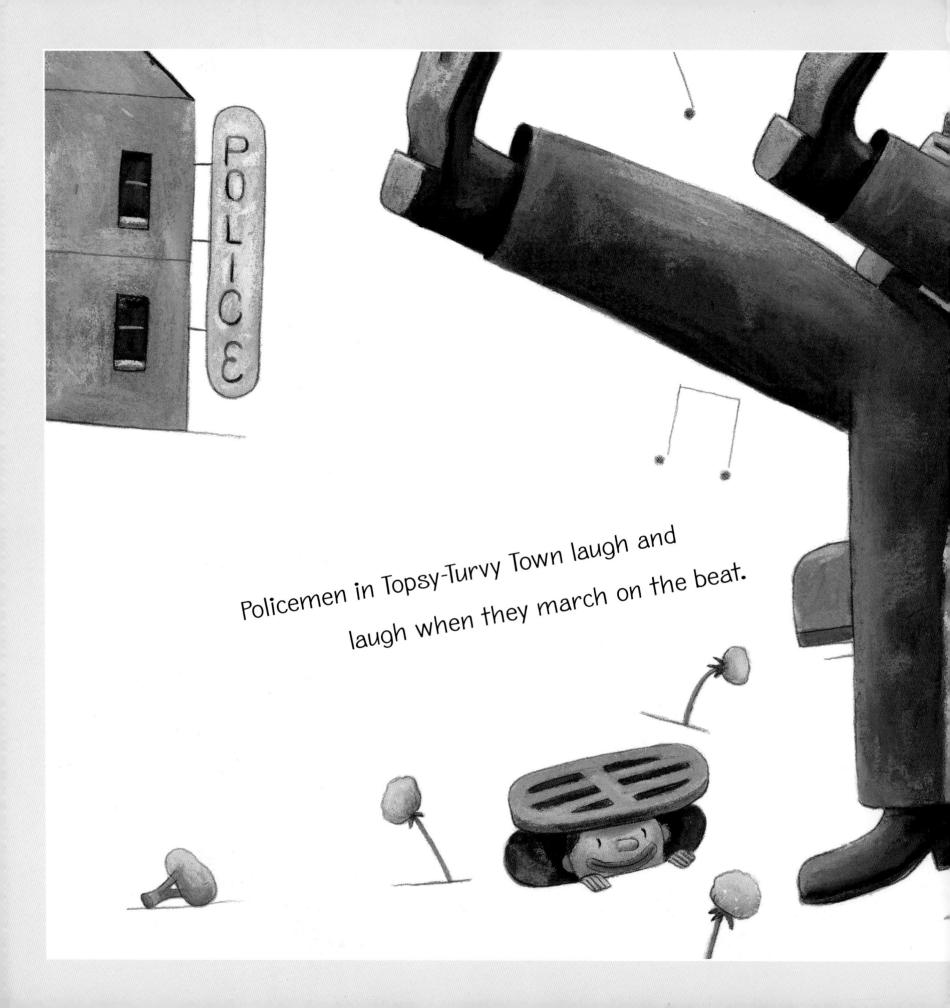

Policemen in Topsy-Turvy Town laugh and laugh when they march on the beat.

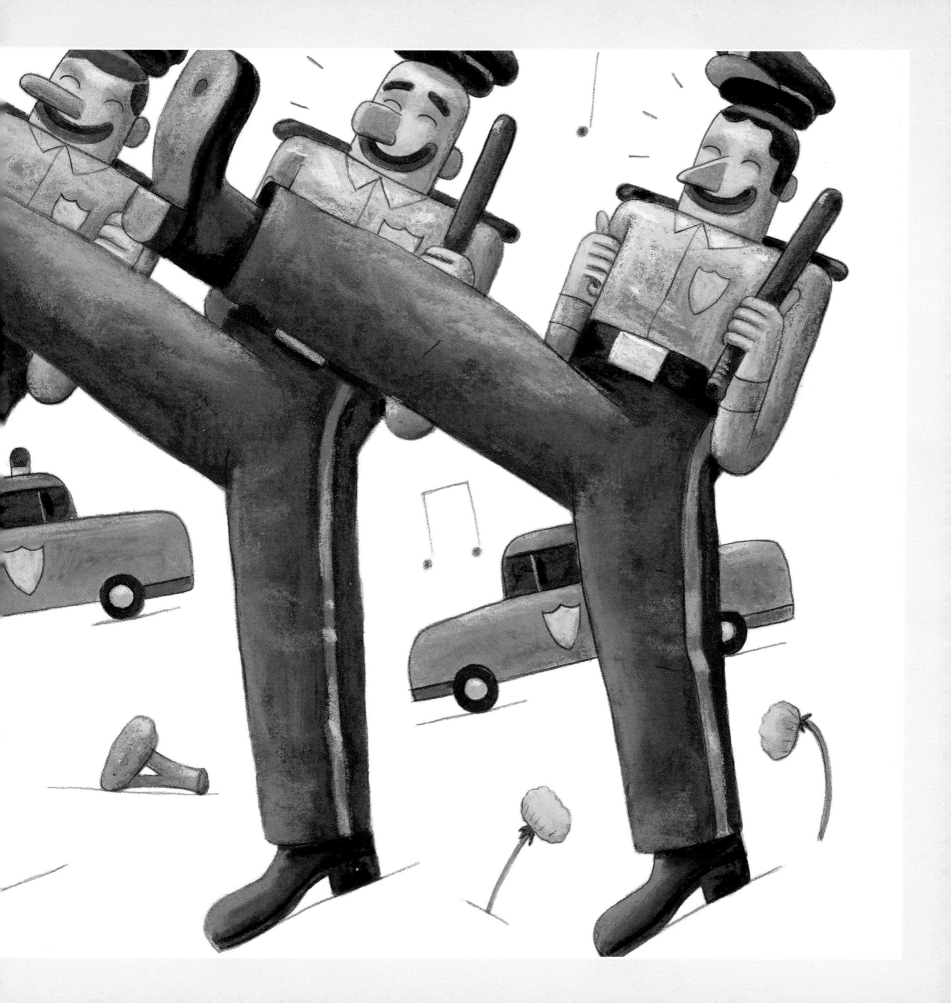

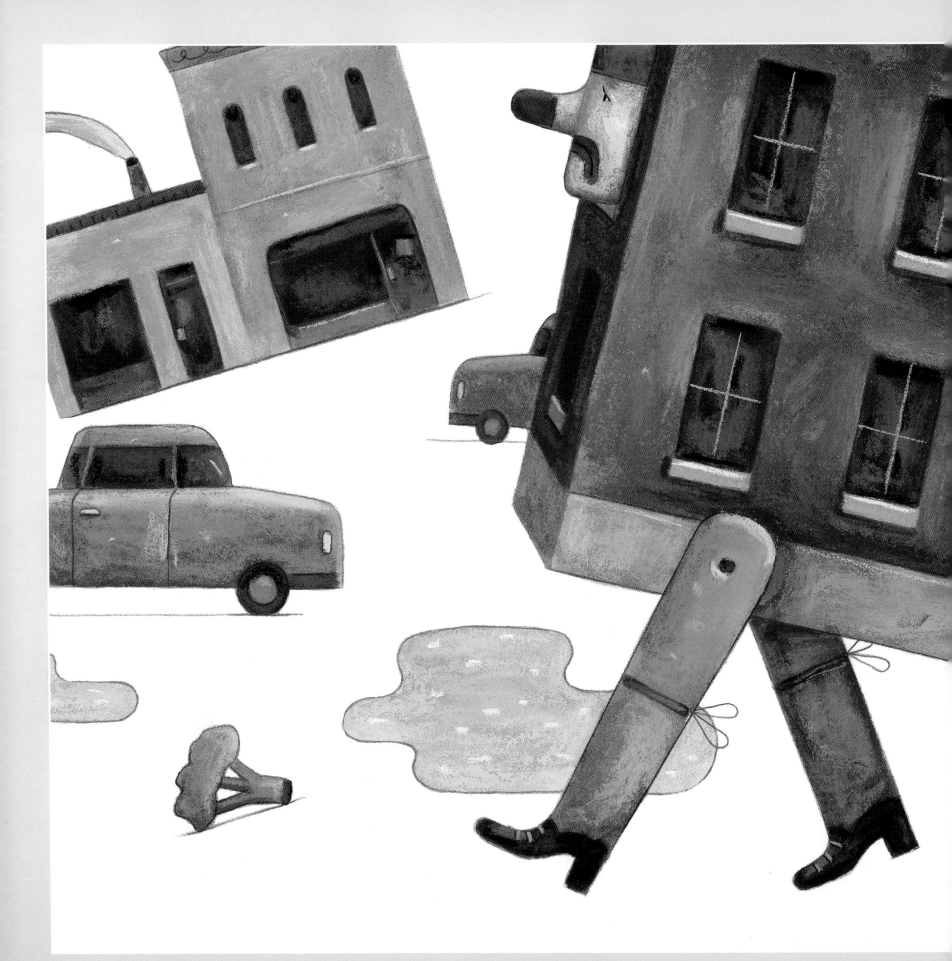

I live in a topsy-turvy neighborhood.
My favorite buildings can come for
a walk with me, if I want them to.
"You're making that up!"
says my aunt.

No, I'm not.
LOOK, THERE'S A POSTMAN
ON A CLOUD!

But I don't say this out loud.

I like living in a topsy-turvy building.

My neighbor Lou has a dog that doesn't bark.

He plays his tuba when he wants Lou to know

it's time to go to the park.

Topsy-turviest of all is our apartment.

You should see who comes to visit me!

Dad pretends to ignore my friends.

When it's dinnertime,
I like my food to be topsy-turvy.
I pretend all the icky and gummy things
are delicious to eat.

After dinner,

I go fishing in the living room.

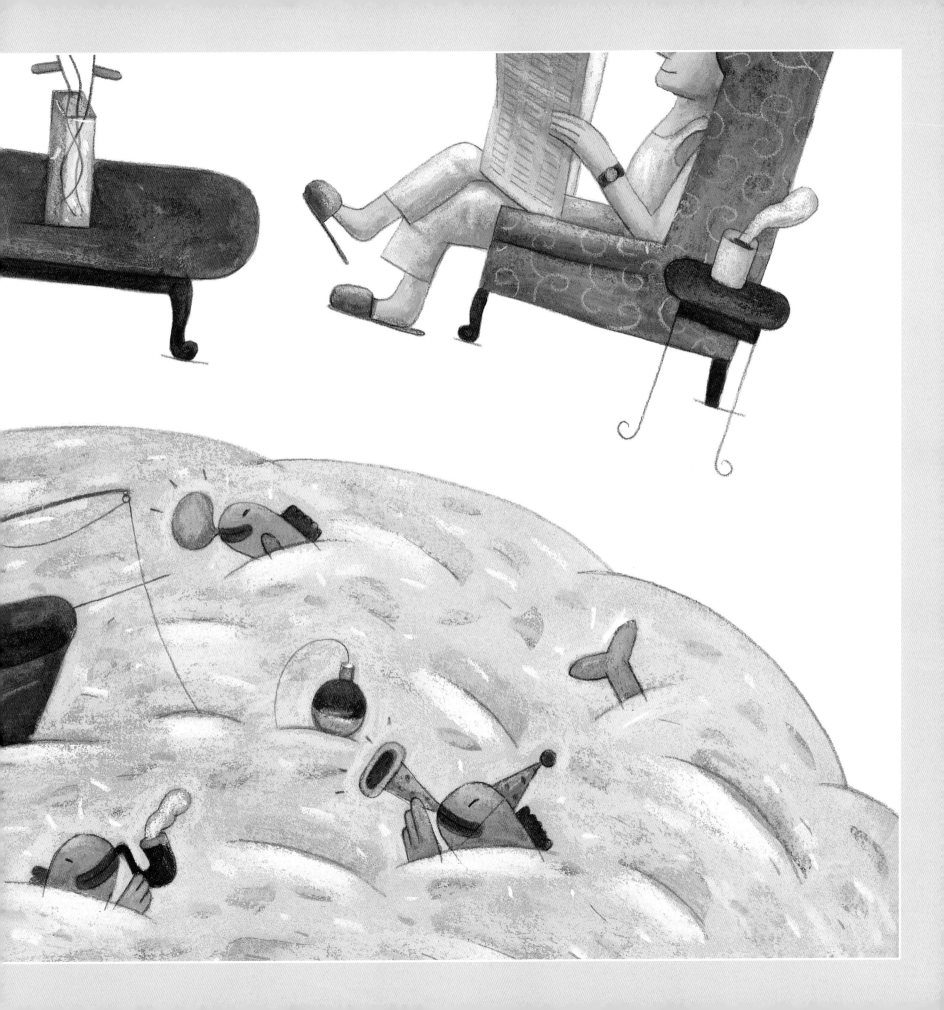

Then I share my bath
with a robot.

And I get ready for bed by juggling a wildcat. "Don't drop him!" cry the others. I never do.

Topsy-Turvy Town lives in my head.
Nobody believes it's there.

Except my mom!